Dedicated to Ruthie

Leroy The Lobster
And Crabby Crab

by

Edward Harriman

Color renderings by Elinor Jaeger from original art by Edward Harriman.
Advice on the language and habits of sea creatures by William Hopkins.

Early one summer morning at Rockland, Maine, the waters of the harbor were calm and crystal clear. The rising sun sent golden shafts from surface to bottom, making the grains of sand shine like tiny diamonds.

Even the seaweed sparkled.

Leroy the Lobster, having finished a hearty breakfast of plankton stew and fried sea fleas, was just leaving his house-in-the-rocks in search of adventure.

No wonder, in all this warm light of the new day, that Leroy should spy, half buried in barnacles and lazy starfish, an old ship's logbook, now partially exposed by the running tide and shifting sands.

Just then, Leroy's friend, Crabby the Crab, came out of his tin-can house to see what Leroy had found.

"Wait a minute, Sonny," he said. "Don't read that old logbook. Something about it gives me a creepy feeling."

"Don't be silly," Leroy said, in a bubble of laughter. "Everything gives crabs a creepy feeling." Then he leaned his back against a discarded truck tire, which was standing in the mud, and began to read the mysterious book.

Suddenly he jumped straight up on his tail. "Look what it says!" he cried.
Crabby crawled closer.

Leroy flip-flapped around and danced on his tail with excitement. "Wow-eee! It says here that a pirate ship laden with treasure was scuttled in Rockland Harbor on a certain night hundreds of years ago. Let me see. Oh, boy! Look! Pieces of eight! Gold and silver! Diamonds and emeralds! Rubies and pearls!"

"By wholloping whiskers, Crabby, old pal, we are going to search for treasure! What a wonderful day for adventure!"

"Oh, dear me," said Crabby. "Now my whole day is ruined. And it was such a lovely morning before all this came up. But I suppose I shall have to go with you. I promised your mother I would look after you. My, my! Let me see. Almost a year ago, the day your mother and father got caught in the lobster pot and couldn't get out . . . Oh, what would they say now?"

"Come on. Quick. Let's pack our lunch and strike off."

Soon they were away, heading offshore, away from their comfortable home in Rockland Harbor.

Leroy flipped and laughed with joy, but not Crabby, for Crabby knew of the dangers ahead. So he kept one eye on Leroy and the other on the deep, dark waters around them.

At last they came to a comfortable spot near the base of the breakwater at the harbor's entrance.

"Whew!" Leroy said, "I'm tired. Let's stop and rest."

"Good idea," Crabby replied, "but we must not waste too much time. You know how quickly the water gets dark after sundown."

"Oh, don't be silly. We've got lots of time left."

"Remember, Leroy, half of our daylight belongs to the trip home. It takes as long to come back as it does to go out. You must listen to me. I am older and wiser than you."

Leroy just laughed.

But he laughed too soon. For at that very moment, appearing from nowhere, flashing past them with a swish of wild water, charged Big Bad Bill the Codfish, the most dreaded enemy of lobsters and crabs, the most savage codfish in Rockland Harbor.

"Help! Help! What shall we do?" cried the frightened Leroy. "He will turn around and come back to grab us both!"

"Quick!" cried Crabby. "Hide here!" He grabbed Leroy with his claw and snatched him quickly behind a heavy growth of thick seaweed.

"Don't move an inch. Here he comes. But he can't find us here."

When Bad Bill finally gave up the hunt and disappeared, Leroy exclaimed, "Whew! That was a close call. I almost shed my shell before it was time. I guess you are right, Crabby. We really must beware of danger when we're as far away from home as this!"

"No matter. We are safe for the moment. Let us be on with the adventure, if you must. Whoops! My, my! Look behind this seaweed! There's a big cave in here!"

"Wow-eee! See how big it is. Crabby, look! What is that strange reflection? Come on. Let's go inside."

"Careful, Leroy. Caves can be dangerous. Proceed with caution."

Slowly they crept inside. And what do you think they found?

You are right. The treasure chest! Pieces of eight! Gold and silver! Diamonds and emeralds! Rubies and pearls!

"Wow-eee! It takes your breath away!" cried Leroy, grabbing at the valuable gems.

"Don't be greedy, Leroy. Just a minute! How did this heavy treasure chest get into this cave?"

"Oh, dear!"

"Right, Leroy. Only one creature could handle a job like this!"

"Awful Austin!"

"Right again. Awful Austin the Awesome Octopus. Awful Austin from southern waters, who summers in Maine! This must be his summer cave. So this must be his treasure. Quick, Leroy. We must get out of here before he returns or surely we —"

"I'm not leaving until I get some of this loot."

Leroy hastily emptied all the food from his sack and began to fill it with jewels.

"Oh, what a stupid thing to do! You have thrown away all our good food. We can't eat diamonds and pearls. We'll starve to death — if Awful Austin doesn't get us first."

Suddenly the water darkened outside the cave.

"Awful Austin! He's coming!"

Swiftly they darted out of the cave, but Leroy had all he could do to swim with his heavy sack of treasure.

And there was Awful Austin coming towards them!

"Oh, what are we going to do?"

"Look, Leroy! There's a school of mackerel swimming up Penobscot Bay. Hurry. We'll hide amongst them. He'll never see us."

Crabby and Leroy were suddenly swept up by the school of mackerel and tumbled along at very high speed through the water.

"Glub! Glub!" Leroy tried to call out something to Crabby, but he couldn't say anything at all.

Maybe they were safe. But, NO! What was that noise? Ka-chug, Ka-chug, Ka-chug! A huge fishing boat was passing overhead.

Suddenly they found themselves packed tightly amongst the mackerel and rising slowly to the surface in the big net of the fishing boat.

"Oh, my goodness! What are we going to do now?" cried Leroy.

"I'm afraid this is the worst mess we ever got into," said Crabby. "I'm afraid this is the end!"

"Oh, merciful heavens!" wailed Leroy.

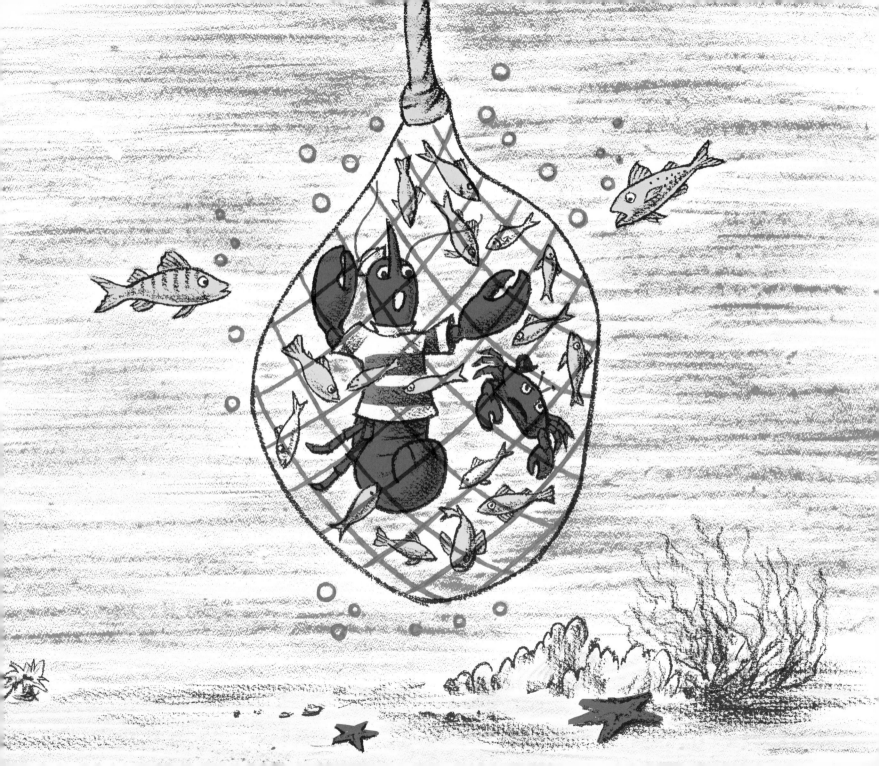

"Hey! There's my old friend, Simon the Sea Turtle, swimming by. Simon! Hey, Simon! Over here! Help! Help!"

Simon the Sea Turtle changed his course and swam towards the big net.

"'Good day, Crabby Crab," croaked Simon, in his slow way. "What in the world are you doing in that thing?"

"We are caught. Help! Help us get out, or surely we are lost forever!"

With one bite of his powerful jaws, Simon ripped a hole in the net. Leroy and Crabby climbed out and dropped back to the ocean bottom with Simon the Sea Turtle quietly following them.

"Simon, old friend, we thank you kindly for saving our lives," said Crabby sincerely.

"What in the world are you doing, so far away from home?"

Leroy told Simon about the adventure.

"Did you manage to save any of the jewels, Leroy?"

Leroy looked into his sack.

"Wow-eee! I still have enough left to buy a million fishegg sandwiches and a brand new house for each of us!"

"Gentlemen, I have an idea," drawled Simon. "You boys are a long way from home. You couldn't possibly get back before dark. But if you don't mind using that diamond bracelet for a collar and that string of pearls for reins, you can harness me up and I will give you a quick ride home on my back."

"Splendid," said Crabby, "no sooner said than done!" And soon they were swirling along at high speed on Simon's back.

When they arrived home, Leroy clicked his claws with joy. "Oh, thank you, Simon, old friend. Crabby and I want you to keep the diamond collar for bringing us safely home."

"Oh, boy," laughed Simon. "Now I am the grandest turtle in the ocean!"

"And for you, Crabby Crab," said Leroy, "I have saved this beautiful diamond ring."

"But what have you saved for yourself?" asked Crabby.

"Why, I still have the beautiful string of pearls, and our happy memories of a great adventure."

Then with a toss of his head, and a smile on his face, Simon the Sea Turtle swam away, waving good-bye to his friends, Leroy the Lobster and Crabby Crab.